Weather

Le temps

leh toh

Illustrated by Clare Beaton

Illustré par Clare Beaton

BARRON'S

rain

la pluie

lah plwee

sun

le soleil

leh sol*ay*

fog

le brouillard

leh broo-*yar*

snow

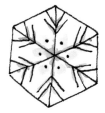

la neige

lah neh-jsh

ice

la glace

lah glahss

wind

le vent

leh voh

cloud

le nuage

leh noo*ah*-jsh

thunder

le tonnerre

leh ton*air*

lightning

les éclairs

lezeh-*clair*

storm

l'orage

lor*ah*-jsh

rainbow

l'arc-en-ciel

larkon-see-*ell*

A simple guide to pronouncing the French words

- Read this guide as naturally as possible, as if it were English.
- Put stress on the letters in *italics*, for example, leh ton*air*.
- Remember that the final consonants in French generally are silent.

la pluie	lah plwee	**rain**
le soleil	leh sol*ay*	**sun**
le brouillard	leh broo-*yar*	**fog**
la neige	lah neh-jsh	**snow**
la glace	lah glahss	**ice**
le vent	leh voh	**wind**
le nuage	leh noo*ah*-jsh	**cloud**
le tonnerre	leh ton*air*	**thunder**
les éclairs	lezeh-*clair*	**lightning**
l'orage	lor*ah*-jsh	**storm**
l'arc-en-ciel	larkon-see-*ell*	**rainbow**

Text and illustrations © Copyright 2001 b small publishing, Surrey, England
First edition for the United States, Canada, and the Philippines published 2001 by Barron's Educational Series, Inc.

Address all inquiries to: Barron's Educational Series, Inc., 250 Wireless Boulevard, Hauppauge, New York 11788
http://www.barronseduc.com
ISBN-13: 978-0-7641-1691-9   ISBN-10: 0-7641-1691-6
Library of Congress Catalog Card Number 00-110625
Printed in China   9876543